Bella, the Late Bloomer

by Liza Charlesworth

ISBN: 978-1-338-89043-3

Designer: Cynthia Ng; Illustrated by John Lund

Copyright © 2023 by Liza Charlesworth. All rights reserved. Published by Scholastic Inc.

1 2 3 4 5 6 7 8 9 10   68   31 30 29 28 27 26 25 24 23 22

Printed in Jiaxing, China. First printing, January 2023.

Once upon a time,
there was a little garden.
In winter, the garden was quiet
and covered in white snow.

But in spring...*POP, POP, POP*!
Little green sprouts began
to poke through the ground.
One of them was named Bella.

3

Bella liked the other sprouts A LOT!
On one side was a sprout named Ron.
Ron told jokes and made Bella laugh.

On the other side was a sprout named Liv.
Liv knew cool stuff about science.
She shared facts that made Bella think.

Bella and Ron and Liv were
BEST, BEST, BEST friends.
They loved to sing in the rain!
They loved to dance in the sun!

Each day, the three sprouts grew.
Ron and Liv grew fast.
They got VERY tall.
But Bella grew slowly.
She stayed quite small.

Then, one sunny day...*POP*!
Ron bloomed into a flower.
He was big and bright
and red as a cherry.
"I'm not a sprout anymore!" he sang.

Then, the next week…*POP*!
Liv bloomed into a flower.
She was big and bright
and blue as a blueberry.
"Look at me!" she said with pride.

Bella watched Ron and Liv
play catch with an acorn.
Throw, catch! Throw, catch!
Bella wanted to play, too,
but she was still too small.

Bella watched Ron and Liv
share a cool book about trees.
Read, read, read!
Bella wanted to read it, too,
but she was still too small.

Bella was happy for her friends,
but she felt jealous, too.
Big tears fell from her eyes.
"When do I get to bloom?" she cried.
A kind bird saw that Bella was sad and said,
"It will happen when the time is right."

So Bella waited and waited.
Each day she grew a little bit.
Then a big rainstorm came
and guess what?
Bella grew a LOT, LOT, LOT!

When the sun came out…*POP*!
The time was FINALLY right.
Bella bloomed into a flower.
She was big and bright
and yellow as a lemon.

Now Bella was just as tall as Ron and Liv.
"Hooray!" they cheered with glee.
"You are all grown up, just like us!"
Then, Bella and her BEST, BEST, BEST friends
played a game of catch.

After that, the pals read an awesome book
about a lion that was a late bloomer.
And every flower in the garden
lived happily ever after!